PURE HUMAN CITY

CLAIRE MILLER

Published in 2016 by Campsie Hills Books

ISBN Paperback: 978-0-9956458-0-6
eBook: 978-0-9956458-1-3

A CIP catalogue copy of this book can be found in the British Library.

Published with the help of Indie Authors World

Dedication

To all my friends and family who have supported me
in the process of producing this book.

Acknowledgements

I'd like to thank Christine McPherson for guiding me in my first time of editing anything I have written. Kim and Sinclair MacLeod at Indie Authors World for helping me through the process of publishing my first book. Friends and family who read my story and given me their honest feedback.

Chapter 1

Kyle hurriedly closed the door announcing his entry to the Library, then paused and waited to see if he could hear footsteps. None came. He didn't really expect to hear any, but he waited just in case.

No-one came to the Library now. They were too busy trying to survive. Life in the Ordinary Settlement was hard. As more people had become Pure Humans, there were fewer hands available to carry out the work needed to provide food and maintain the buildings. There was an air of neglect and uncaring. The inside of the Library looked just like the Ordinary Settlement – dust coated the books abandoned on the tables, and paint had peeled off the walls.

Kyle briefly wondered why he lived in a place called the Ordinary Settlement while the Pure Humans lived in the Pure Human City. He let the thought go. He had other things to think about – like why he was in the Library in the first place. He paused again just to be sure that no-one was coming.

He wasn't really supposed to be there. It wasn't exactly forbidden, but it wasn't encouraged either. There was an attitude from the adults of 'leave well alone' and 'just get on with day-to-day life'. Kyle wasn't sure what the adults thought was so scary about books. They were just books, weren't they?

He had tried talking to his parents about the Pure Oxygen Machines and the Pure Human City, but they always changed the subject. They said that he should be content to live where he was and to be who he was. *Being who he was*, he wondered, *what did that mean?* He hoped to find some answers to his questions in the Library.

For as long as he had lived, there had always been the Pure Human City. People from the Ordinary Settlement went there and never returned; they were never mentioned by anyone in the Ordinary Settlement again. Whatever happened to them, his parents made sure he didn't see.

There was an Office of the Organisation who provided the Pure Oxygen Machines in the Ordinary Settlement, if you wanted one, but Kyle had never been there and wouldn't dare. His parents would be so angry, it wasn't worth it. They were startlingly clear on one thing: a Pure Oxygen Machine would never be allowed in their home.

Kyle turned his attention back to the Library. He had to start his search somewhere, but where? He surveyed the scene in front of him. The main room was square with doors coming off at regular intervals. *Private reading rooms,* he guessed. The windows, high on the walls, streamed dust-speckled light. He suppressed a cough quickly, as the dust he had disturbed by entering settled. *Well,* he thought, *I'll start with the first reading room and work my way round the walls.*

He walked past the shelves of disregarded books which clung to the walls between the doors. Slowly he pushed the door open, fearful of what he might find. He half expected to find someone in there, who would look up from their book and either scowl or smile. There was no-one there.

The window opposite the door showed a table with several books scattered on it. One, facing towards the window, was lying open at a page. Kyle walked round, curious to know what was being read. Carefully he brushed his hand across the pages. Dust moved away to reveal faded words. They were difficult to make out. The light over the years had faded the ink to almost nothing. He just about made out the word 'glorious', but that was all. Whatever had been glorious, Kyle would never know.

He looked up to the rest of the room. The walls were bare, empty of anything. He had half expected to find posters showing pictures of books to read, or events to come. He wondered what had happened that his parents and all the other adults had abandoned the Library and decided never to allow the children to go there. Certainly, he had never been here before. His parents had always read to him and given him books at home, but they had never encouraged him to come to the Library. In fact, the place was never mentioned.

He shrugged his shoulders. No matter, he thought, he had information to find. He went back into the main room and explored several other reading rooms, but found the same thing. It was frustrating and curious at the same time. He had no idea how he was going to find or even know when he was looking at the information he wanted. What if it was too faded for him to read?

Deciding to be systematic, he searched all the remaining reading rooms. Having found nothing, he set about searching the tables, hoping he would have better luck.

The books on the tables hadn't faded so badly, so Kyle was able to read them. Some were really interesting, and he found himself reading a little in each of the books he came across. He loved reading, and wondered once again what had happened to make the adults abandon the Library. There were so many unknown books around the walls.

The change in the light coming through the windows alerted Kyle that the day was getting on. He could only stay for so long before his parents would miss him. They mustn't know he had come to the Library. He was going to find his information, even if it meant having to come back and search again.

There was time to look on one last table. There he discovered more dust and more slightly faded words.

His search was quicker than before, as he was now aware of the time. He had to leave the Library… now.

Pushing aside a heavy tome, he glimpsed a smooth, shiny, dust-free book cover. Hurriedly, he shoved the top book aside, eager to see what was underneath. *'The Origins of Paradise'* declared itself. He had to leave.

Quickly he covered it up with a few other books, just in case someone else was to come into the Library. Kyle was the only one who was going to read *'The Origins of Paradise'*.

He raced down the street, passing the scattered ruins of homes that had once been lived in. These were the homes of people who had become Pure Humans and gone to live in the Pure Human City.

Ruined and lived-in houses sat side-by-side around the fields where the food was grown for the Ordinary Settlement. That was where he was heading now. His house was right beside the fields. He jumped to avoid a rut in the road. The last thing he needed was to get injured. Then his parents would definitely want to know where he had been.

Kyle passed the Office of the Organisation – the only building in the Ordinary Settlement that looked cared for. Its brickwork positively gleamed. On a bright day, sunlight seemed to bounce off the outside walls. Away on the outskirts of the Ordinary Settlement sat the Pure Human City. Kyle could just see the top of the dome from where he stood. He had only ever seen it from a distance; his parents had made sure of that.

He dodged through the houses and saw his parents just finishing in the field nearest his home. They would never know where he had been, he thought with relief. He ducked quickly into the doorway of his house, just before his parents were about to reach him.

- - -

Several days passed before Kyle was able to return to the Library. His parents had kept him busy in the fields, almost as if they knew he had been somewhere he wasn't meant to be. They kept giving him sideways glances, and he just hoped he didn't look too guilty.

He closed the Library door behind himself slower this time. First, to reduce the ear-splitting creaking it made when it opened, and second, to reduce the dust cloud created when the door closed. Nothing had changed. Nevertheless, Kyle waited just a moment in case anyone else was in the Library.

The book was exactly where he had left it, buried under all the dust-covered books. He stared at it for several minutes, and then he slowly ran his hand over the cover. It was totally smooth. *What,* he wondered, *was so different about this book that no dust had settled on it? Who had put it in the Library?* Questions flooded his mind. There was only one way to find out. He opened the book.

Chapter 2

The gleam from the pages made him blink for several minutes. The words seemed to dance across the page. He had never seen a book like this before; he needed to know more. He carried on blinking until his vision cleared.

There was a picture of a silver cube on the page, with the words **'Your future assured with our Pure Oxygen Machine'** above it. *So this was a Pure Oxygen Machine,* he thought. He was sure he had overheard his parents talking about small silver cubes before. It looked very exciting. He took a breath, realising he had been holding it in his excitement. He was finally going to find out what he wanted to know.

'Turn over,' the words under the silver cube announced, 'to discover your route to perfect health and happiness.'

With shaking hands, he turned the page. A picture of a person smiling filled the top half of the page. Kyle guessed it was an Organisation Rep. Kyle had seen them, from a distance, coming out of the Office of the

Organisation. His parents had always made sure that was as close as he ever got.

His parents behaved very oddly sometimes. *The Organisation Reps looked just like anyone in the Ordinary Settlement, Kyle thought. Why did he need to be kept away from them?*

'Our Organisation Reps are here to guide you,' the book started, 'to total health and happiness. They have placed this book in your Library to inform your decision about having a Pure Oxygen Machine in your home, and will answer any questions you may have. We know you will make the right choice.'

'This book, made from a special material of our own construction, will enable you to always be able to read our information, to choose the way to perfect health.'

Kyle thought all books should be made of this material, then he would be able to read them all without faded ink.

'We are offering you an opportunity,' the book continued, 'to enhance your feeling of wellbeing. The trees are producing oxygen in the Ordinary Settlement, but is it enough? We think you need more. Our Pure Oxygen Machines are just the answer you are looking for. The extra oxygen our Pure Oxygen Machines provide will boost your vitality. Your energy levels will increase. You will feel an endless source of ability to do whatever you want to do. Just talk to our Organisation Rep and they can arrange for an immediate installation of a Pure Oxygen Machine in your home.'

Kyle thought this all sounded wonderful. His parents came home from the fields tired every night. Just think how much better they would feel if they had the extra oxygen from a Pure Oxygen Machine. He dived back into the book to see what else it had to say.

'An additional benefit is our Pure Human City. You will be a Pure Human with our Oxygen and, after a qualifying period, you will be eligible to join us there. We promise a high quality of life with no stresses. All we ask in return is a small amount of work. You won't regret getting a Pure Oxygen Machine. We're ready to welcome you to our family.'

Kyle wanted to run straight out of the Library and head to the Pure Human City. The life sounded wonderful. But he knew his parents wouldn't allow it. He would have to find a way to get to the Pure Human City without them ever finding out. That would be tricky. He also had no idea, having never been allowed near there, how to get in. Somehow he knew he had to find out what he needed to know.

The book gave him the answer immediately. 'When you are ready to join us, all you have to do is come to the entrance of the Pure Human City. You will find the Pure Human City on the other side of the woods, next to the Ordinary Settlement boundary. We will scan you to ensure you are qualified to enter the Pure Human City. We want you to be ready to fully enjoy your life with us. All you have to do is come and join us.'

'You will see our forcefield surrounding the Pure Human City. It's there for your protection. We want you to feel safe and secure. You will come to no harm when you are with us.'

Kyle realised the dome he could see from a distance must be the forcefield. He wondered what it looked like close-up, and why the Pure Humans needed to be protected. He was sure to find out when he got to the Pure Human City.

He turned his attention back to the book. 'Come see what awaits you in the Pure Human City,' it announced.

A picture of the Pure Human City was on the page. The description underneath read, 'Here is your first sight of what awaits you when you join us.'

Kyle stared in wonder. What struck him most was the whiteness of the single-storey buildings and the roads. The buildings lined the streets, which radiated out from the bottom of the picture leading further into the Pure Human City. Light shone off the walls of the buildings and roads just like the pages of *The Origins of Paradise*. Kyle imagined touching the buildings' walls and finding them as smooth as the book cover. The buildings looked just like the houses in the Ordinary Settlement in shape, but he wanted to find out what it would be like to live in the Pure Human City.

Kyle guessed the people pictured standing in groups in front of some of the houses must be Pure Humans. They were smiling and looking very happy. Kyle's parents were always tired and worried. He wanted to be able to make his parents smile like the

Pure Humans. Going to the Pure Human City was looking like the solution he had been searching for.

The next picture was labelled 'Organisation Headquarters'. The Organisation Headquarters was a tall building, and another group of smiling people were pictured standing outside. He read the description. 'Here is the Organisation Headquarters with our Organisation Reps. They are ready to help you at all times and can't wait to meet you.'

Kyle thought the Organisation Reps looked just like the adults in the Ordinary Settlement and the Pure Humans. He wasn't sure how he was going to tell the Pure Humans and the Organisation Reps apart.

The next picture showed a white wall with an open doorway cut into it. There was a sign above the doorway which said 'Work Place'. 'Here,' the description explained, 'is where you will carry out your work. Each of you will do work you are most suitable for – no more doing what you don't want to do.'

This sounded extremely appealing to Kyle. He didn't really want to work in the fields with his parents, but had no option. He wondered what his mum and dad would like to do if they had the choice.

The last picture showed another white wall with an open doorway cut into it, like the previous photograph. The words above the doorway this time said 'Recreation Centre'. The description read, 'Here you can relax and enjoy spending time together.' The Organisation had thought of everything, Kyle realised. Life in the Pure Human City seemed perfect.

Kyle rapidly came to the conclusion that life in the Pure Human City had to be better than in the Ordinary Settlement. He was going to go there and see it for himself. Then he would persuade his parents that they all needed to be there.

He had reached the end of the book.

'We have shown you what is possible with a Pure Oxygen Machine,' the book concluded. 'We look forward to welcoming you to our family in the Pure Human City soon.'

Kyle closed the book, his mind full of thoughts of how to get to the Pure Human City. He hid it under the dusty old books again, and then left the Library. He wandered towards his home deep in thought, barely noticing his parents leaving the fields as he reached his front door.

- - -

An opportunity presented itself unexpectedly one morning, just a few days later. Kyle was about to join his parents in the fields when they announced that an Ordinary Settlement meeting had been called. This meant that the adults disappeared for several hours. The children were never invited to these meetings, and the older children looked after those too young to look after themselves. Kyle was old enough to be left on his own, so his parents told him to amuse himself and keep out of trouble, then left.

Kyle watched them leave the house until he could no longer see them. Once he was certain they had gone, he left the house.

Chapter 3

H e slid out of the front door. Checked no-one had spotted him. Remembered to breathe. There was no-one near him. Creeping slowly forward, he made his way through the surrounding houses, all the time aware of his racing heartbeat.

Kyle's thoughts went back to what *'The Origins of Paradise'* had said about where the Pure Human City was and how to get into it.

He had to go to the Ordinary Settlement boundary, then through the wood separating the Ordinary Settlement and the Pure Human City.

It seemed to take forever to reach the boundary. He was being so careful, he felt his heart was about to burst out of his chest. He had never gone to the boundary before; some adult would have told his parents if he had tried to do it. But now here he was, on the verge of a life-changing adventure.

Excited and scared all at once, Kyle couldn't wait to see the Pure Human City. He just knew it was where his parents needed to be. At the same time he was scared of what they would say when they found out he had gone there. He would have to tell them if he was going to persuade them to go there. He decided not to worry about that just now. His parents would understand once he explained what he had learned.

With his heart thumping, he headed into the woods. A quick look round told him no- one was behind him.

At first he trod carefully, making sure his feet avoided the branches on the ground. The further he moved into the wood the braver he became, moving with more confidence. He was running by the time he reached the other side of the wood.

He stopped and leaned on a tree, breathing heavily, looking out at the forcefield which stood in the middle of the clearing in front of him. It looked enormous. It seemed to Kyle to grow from the ground and reach high into the sky. The air around the forcefield shimmered. He couldn't see through it.

A line of people were standing by the base of the forcefield – some he recognised from the Ordinary Settlement, others he didn't. Kyle reasoned they had to be Pure Humans.

He couldn't see any way in. This puzzled him, as *'The Origins of Paradise'* had clearly told the Pure Humans to come to the entrance of the Pure Human City. Frustrated, he waited to see what was going to happen. The Pure Humans obviously wanted to get in, too.

As he watched, the forcefield parted at the base, revealing a glimpse of white. This had to be the entrance. Kyle raced from where he stood to join the Pure Humans waiting to get into the Pure Human City.

Attempting to collect his breath as quickly as possible, he waited with them, hoping he would recover in time before they went into the Pure Human City. They hadn't been running like Kyle, and he couldn't afford to stand out. Compared to him, they were all calm, quiet, and waiting patiently. They all wore the same odd smile on their faces. Kyle couldn't say why, but he thought something just wasn't quite right about them.

As one, the group of Pure Humans moved forward. Kyle huddled at the back, sticking close to the one in front of him. He had to blink hard as the group went into the Pure Human City; the white light dazzled his eyes.

The group waited quietly in an area just inside the forcefield. Kyle saw the entrance close over, followed by two people coming towards them with boxes in their hands. These had to be the Organisation Reps, he realised.

The boxes in their hands had to be the scanners, and he panicked as he remembered what *'The Origins of Paradise'* had said about the Pure Humans being scanned when they entered the Pure Human City. If they got to him, they would know he wasn't a Pure Human. *What was he going to do?* Out of the corner of his eye he spotted a nearby building. He ducked quickly behind it.

His eyes had adjusted to the light by this time, and he peered carefully round the building to see the Organisation Reps placing the scanners on the Pure Humans' outstretched hands. The Organisation Reps didn't look his way. He hadn't been noticed.

He took a deep breath, relieved he had made it safely into the Pure Human City. Getting out was going to be interesting, but that was something to think about later. Now he was inside, and he had some exploring to do.

Chapter 4

The Organisation Reps finished scanning all the Pure Humans' hands. Without any words being spoken, they turned away from the group of Pure Humans and began walking along one of the roads. The group of Pure Humans followed. Kyle noticed the Pure Humans didn't ask anything or question the Organisation Reps. It was as if they were following instructions. The Organisation Reps appeared to be making all the decisions; Kyle realised he was going to have to be very careful whilst he was in the Pure Human City.

He was desperate to know what was going to happen to the Pure Humans, but couldn't risk being seen. As the single-storey buildings lining the road were relatively close together, Kyle judged he could, if he was careful, move behind the buildings and keep up with the group. The buildings would give him cover from the Organisation Reps if he needed it.

He set off, ducking behind each building as the group moved up the road. His breathing was loud in his ears. His pulse was beginning to race. He was sure the Organisation Reps must have heard him.

The group moved up the road past several buildings until the Organisation Reps stopped. The group of Pure Humans stopped, too. They seemed to know exactly when to move and stop. Kyle found this very puzzling when no-one had said a word.

The Pure Humans kept smiling. They hadn't talked since coming into the Pure Human City, nor had they talked whilst waiting to get through the forcefield. He had assumed the Pure Humans would talk because that was what the people in the Ordinary Settlement did. Compared to the Pure Human City, the Ordinary Settlement was positively a riot of sound.

Peeking round the edge of a building, Kyle saw the Pure Humans split into small groups. The groups moved to the nearest buildings and went into them. Once they were all inside, the Organisation Reps walked away along the road. They never looked back, obviously expecting the Pure Humans to do as they had been instructed. Kyle still couldn't figure out how those instructions had been communicated.

He watched, fascinated. How did the Pure Humans know which group to get into? How did the groups know which buildings to go into? He needed some answers. Making sure that the Organisation Reps had gone, he made his way to the front of the nearest building and looked at it properly for the first time. *'The Origins of Paradise'* had shown the buildings shaped like those in the Ordinary Settlement. Here the buildings were square with an opening at the front; there were no windows. Kyle didn't understand why 'The Origins of Paradise' would show one thing when the reality was different. He peered in through the open doorway.

The group of Pure Humans were standing in a circle, silently smiling at each other. Kyle crept forward to see exactly what was going on. He had to be careful not to let the Pure Humans know he was there. He didn't want to be discovered and flung out of the Pure Human City because he wasn't a Pure Human, but the group gave no indication that they knew he was there.

Going as close as he dared to the circle, he peered through the gaps between the Pure Humans. In the middle of the circle was a small silver cube, which seemed to hover above a silver pillar resting on the ground. A Pure Oxygen Machine; Kyle recognised it from 'The Origins of Paradise'. Not one of the Pure Humans moved. Kyle wasn't sure they were breathing, either, but daren't get too close to find out.

This all seemed odd to Kyle, and certainly not the lifestyle he had in mind for his parents. The thought of never hearing his mother's voice again was unthinkable. *What was going on?*

He stood and stared at the group of Pure Humans for several minutes. They stayed the same, neither moving nor speaking; all they did was smile. Uncomfortable, Kyle quickly left the building.

Outside, he leant his back against the wall, trying to make sense of what he had just seen. Something was nagging in his thoughts. Something was wrong with the building.

Suddenly he realised what was bothering him. There had been light coming from somewhere, but the building had no windows. Reluctantly, he went in again, this time staring at the walls of the building. Light seemed to be coming from somewhere but he wasn't sure how. It certainly wasn't through any windows. Spooked, he rushed back out of the building.

One by one, he went into all of the buildings, and found it was the same in every case. Each group of Pure Humans stood in a circle around a Pure Oxygen Machine, smiling at each other.

Kyle had been worried that a Pure Human might recognise him and tell the Organisation Reps he was in the Pure Human City, but he didn't think that would happen now. He felt like he was the only real person in the world at the moment. He wanted to see his mum and dad. To tell them he loved them.

He paused to think. He could go back to the entrance and find his way out. This idea seemed extremely appealing. Or he could carry on exploring and see if he could find out any more useful information. Something to take back to his parents to prove that he had the best of intentions and really wanted to help them. Maybe he could find out how to reverse whatever was happening to the people who had become Pure Humans.

He decided to go on. But where? If he followed the road, he might possibly find the Organisation Headquarters. There he would be able, he was sure, to find out what he needed to know. He checked the road was clear.

As he walked along the road, he looked into the buildings he passed. Some were empty but most had a group of Pure Humans standing in a circle around a Pure Oxygen Machine. He shivered. He didn't like this at all.

'The Origins of Paradise' had mentioned nothing about all of this. Kyle now realised why there was a forcefield around the Pure Human City. No-one would have a Pure Oxygen Machine in their home if they knew this was going to happen to them. The forcefield was protecting the Organisation, not the Pure Humans.

The road ahead began to curve to the right. Kyle was so focussed on this that he didn't see a Pure Human coming out of a building near to him. He jumped back in fright, stifling a scream. He couldn't afford to be discovered. But the Pure Human carried on walking as if Kyle wasn't there. Another Pure Human passed Kyle, then another.

Around him, the buildings were all emptying of their Pure Humans; all wearing the same fixed smile on their faces. Kyle followed them, curious to see where they were going next.

The end of the road came out onto an empty space which Kyle would have called a meeting place, if there had been anyone to meet up with.

The tall building of the Organisation Headquarters dominated the area. It was just as it was pictured in *'The Origins of Paradise'*. Adjoining the Headquarters on either side was a white wall. The left side had an open doorway with the sign above it saying, 'Work Place'. The right side had an open doorway with a sign above it saying, 'Recreation Centre'. Kyle remembered these doorways and signs from 'The Origins of Paradise'.

He watched as the Pure Humans divided themselves up between the 'Work Place' and the 'Recreation Centre', moving purposefully as though they knew exactly where to go.

Kyle couldn't stand still. He really wanted to go and see what was in the 'Work Place', the 'Recreation Centre', and the Organisation Headquarters. He had to decide quickly. The Organisation Headquarters was first. Then he would go to the 'Work Place', and finally the 'Recreation Centre'.

Trying to move like the Pure Humans, he headed towards the Organisation Headquarters. He looked around to check for Organisation Reps, aware now they would be behaving like him rather than like the Pure Humans. No-one seemed to be taking any interest in him.

When he neared the front of the Organisation Headquarters, he looked around to check no-one was looking at him then slipped through the open doorway in the front of the building.

He pressed his back against the interior wall, consciously breathing. Now all he had to do was find out the information he wanted without being caught by an Organisation Rep. Easy, really. Or so he hoped.

His thoughts were haunted by the smiling faces of all the Pure Humans he'd seen. They were like mindless living robots.

Using his hands, he pushed himself away from the wall. It felt as smooth as the cover of 'The Origins of Paradise'. He shivered.

He had been right in thinking the walls of the buildings would be like the cover of 'The Origins of Paradise', but not about anything else. This adventure was turning into a nightmare – one he was beginning to regret getting into. The Pure Human City was one place he hoped his parents would never come. He turned his attention back to his surroundings.

He was standing in an area empty of anything except a set of stairs at the far end. The stairs hugged the wall and led upwards to the other levels of the building. The walls were similar to those in the single-storey buildings Kyle had seen earlier – white, windowless, but emitting light. Kyle felt very exposed. If an

Organisation Rep came along now, he had nowhere to hide.

He took a deep breath. It was now or never. As confidently as he could, he headed towards the stairs. He was going to look as if he was meant to be there.

The stairs led to a landing. Corridors stretched away to his left and right; the stairs continued up to his immediate right. He paused. Did he continue up, or explore this floor? He decided to stay on this floor, as there was a shorter distance to the exit if he was discovered. The left corridor was nearest.

Creeping slowly round the corner, he saw the corridor for the first time. At first glance it looked like two smooth walls meeting in a dead end; Kyle had expected to see doors leading into rooms. From the outside, the Organisation Headquarters looked too big to be just blank corridors, so where were the rooms?

Inching his way along the wall, he still couldn't see any doors. Halfway along, he heard footsteps. He panicked. There was nowhere to go.

As he pressed his hand into the wall, it slid away revealing an entrance. Kyle jumped into the gap and pressed himself against the nearest wall, praying the footsteps would go past him. The outer wall slid back into place.

Kyle could no longer hear the footsteps; in fact, he couldn't hear anything. He slowly let out the breath he realised he had been holding, relieved he hadn't been discovered. Looking around the windowless room he saw, standing in a corner, what must be a Pure Human. He stood smiling and doing nothing else, like the Pure Humans Kyle had seen in the rest of the Pure Human City. The Pure Human didn't give any sign he had noticed him.

Kyle turned to find the doorway, then remembered the wall had slid across, closing the gap while he had been listening for the footsteps. He was alone in this room with the Pure Human, with no idea where the doorway was or how to open it. He was stuck. His parents would never find him here, once they realised he was missing. He was never going to see them again.

Frantically, he pressed his hands against the wall he had been leaning against. Nothing happened. The wall stayed solid.

Kyle's breath came fast. He was going to die, he just knew it. The Organisation Reps would find him then force him to stand around a Pure Oxygen Machine. He would turn into a Pure Human. He would be changed forever and be as good as dead to his parents.

Tears stung his eyes. Why did he have to be so curious? *Would his parents miss him*, he wondered? Would he be forgotten like all the other people from the Ordinary Settlement who came to the Pure Human City?

He sank miserably into his thoughts. This really was his last adventure. His parents had been right when they had warned him not to go into the Library; look where it had got him. This time there was no way out for him. He slumped to the floor, his back against the wall, and stared at his feet.

After sometime, he turned to face the Pure Human, wondering what – if anything – he would be thinking. Kyle wished he could ask how to leave this room, but any humanity seemed to have been taken away from the Pure Human.

As if answering Kyle's thought, the Pure Human moved to the wall where the entrance had been. As he did, the wall slid across to reveal the doorway. Kyle wasn't sure where the wall slid into; it just seemed to melt into the rest of the wall.

Kyle saw the back of someone standing in the doorway. The Pure Human moved forward out of the room and the other person followed the Pure Human out.

As he heard their footsteps walk away from the room, Kyle took his chance to leave, too. Ahead of him, he saw the person lead the Pure Human down to the dead end of the corridor, away from Kyle. It had to be an Organisation Rep. Neither the Pure Human nor the Organisation Rep looked back.

Kyle saw the Organisation Rep approach the dead end wall, and a doorway outline appeared. On the right a luminous circle became visible. The Organisation Rep placed their right hand on the luminous circle and the wall slid away to reveal another room. The Organisation Rep and Pure Human entered the room, the wall sliding across behind them. The doorway outline and luminous circle disappeared.

Kyle immediately went back to the stairs. He wanted to explore further but didn't fancy getting caught in another room. He had better leave before he really got stuck. He had just put his foot on the first step leading downwards when he heard footsteps coming up the stairs. He had to hide. A glance along the right and left corridors told him there was nowhere there. He headed up the stairs as quietly as he could; there was nowhere else to go.

At the second landing, he stopped. The footsteps didn't follow. Relieved, he leant against the stairway wall. This was turning out to be some adventure.

He looked around him. The corridor to the right was the same as on the first floor. The left corridor had the wall on its right as solid. The wall to the left was broken up by openings. Despite himself, Kyle crept along the wall to see what was in the rooms.

The first room was empty. The second had a Pure Human in it. The third had a couple of desks, with chairs behind them, made from the same materials as the walls. A Pure Human was there, too.

Kyle hesitated. He wanted to go in, but he didn't want to get trapped like last time. What should he do? A luminous circle was visible on the right of the opening. *Maybe if he placed his hand on the luminous circle,* he thought, *he would be able to close the door and open it.* He had to try.

Cautiously, he pressed his hand on the luminous circle. The wall slid shut. Kyle took a breath. The doorway outline and the luminous circle were still visible. He pressed his hand on the luminous circle. The door slid open. He stepped inside and prayed he was correct. He placed his hand on the luminous circle visible to the right of the doorway. The door slid shut. His hand was trembling. At least this time he knew how to get out of the room.

He headed towards the desks. As he reached them, he turned to the Pure Human. He had never studied one close up properly. *Now was as good as time as any*, he thought. At least then he could tell his parents what the signs of a person turning into a Pure Human were.

Kyle touched the Pure Human's arm. It felt as smooth as the cover of *'The Origins of Paradise'*. He stared in shock at the Pure Human. What had been done to this person? Kyle touched the arm again. As well as smooth, it was cold. Kyle noticed it shone like the light coming from the walls of the buildings. He took a step back. The Pure Human just kept smiling and looking ahead.

Kyle was just about to check if the Pure Human was breathing when he noticed the wall beginning to slide open. He dived behind one of the desks.

Peeking cautiously out from behind the desk, he saw two people standing in front of the Pure Human, their backs to him. Kyle tried to breathe quietly.

The two people turned and looked at each other. Their eyes flashed green. They both smiled. As one, they turned to the Pure Human and pushed the Pure Human into the wall. The wall melted around the Pure Human, swallowing him up.

Kyle put his hand over his mouth to stop himself from crying out. The Pure Human had willingly stepped into the wall! Kyle couldn't believe what he had just seen. He knew from the number of houses his parents wouldn't let him near that more people were joining the Pure Humans every day. Soon there would be only a few people left in the Ordinary Settlement. Kyle had to do something to stop this.

The green glint in the Organisation Reps' eyes had shown Kyle how to recognise them from the Pure Humans and the people from the Ordinary Settlement. He had also now seen at first hand the difference in behaviours between the Organisation Reps and the Pure Humans, so he felt more confident he could tell who was who.

As the two Organisation Reps left the room, closing the door behind them, Kyle stared at where the Pure Human had been swallowed by the wall. He had no idea how to feel. Numb; mixed with horror perhaps. He definitely had to find out what the Organisation was up to now.

He looked at the top of the desk where he was hiding. A book with a cover just like 'The Origins of Paradise' lay there. He placed it on the floor beside him to read, ensuring that he wouldn't be instantly visible if any more Organisation Reps came in.

The room, like all the others, was windowless, but the light from the walls was bright enough for Kyle to be able to read the book.

He couldn't help but look up to see if any eyes were watching him from the wall. There weren't. He shivered at the thought of the Pure Human being part of the wall. The sooner he read this book the better.

Chapter 6

The title was *'Operations Manual'*. The book cover felt as smooth as *'The Origins of Paradise'*, which was as smooth as the walls of the buildings, which were as smooth as the arm of the Pure Human.

Kyle's hand jumped away from the cover. The thought that it might actually be part of a Pure Human gave him a fright. He didn't know if he could touch it now. He needed to stop for a moment.

Could he touch the book again? He decided he had to. He had no choice. Gingerly, with the tips of his fingers, he opened the cover to reveal the first page.

There were a number of headings: Ordinary Settlement; Pure Humans; Organisation Reps; Pure Human City; Pure Oxygen Machines; and Organisation Aims.

Kyle had no idea where to start. He paused. Time seemed to stand still. He gave himself a mental shake. He wouldn't find anything out by staring at the headings; he just had to do it. He turned the next page over to the Ordinary Settlement section and started to read.

'We have placed *"The Origins of Paradise"* in the Library to encourage the people of the Ordinary Settlement to want a Pure Oxygen Machine. Some people are particularly easily fooled. The success rate has been very high.'

'There are some people who have resisted us. If they haven't chosen to have a Pure Oxygen Machine by the time our plans have come to the completion stage, they will be rounded up and forcibly converted. The people on this Planet are an excellent quality of stock. When the completion stage has been reached, *"The Origins of Paradise"* will be removed from the Library.'

Kyle was shocked. He couldn't believe what he had just read. The Organisation was treating the people of the Ordinary Settlement like objects, to be owned and used as it saw fit. *What was the Organisation? Where had it come from?*

Kyle turned to the next section, Pure Humans.

'Pure Humans are converted people from the Ordinary Settlement. The Pure Oxygen Machines change the people into our miners. They mine the rocks/minerals we need. They can be totally controlled by the Organisation Reps through thought.'

'The following changes will be observed by the Organisation Rep in the Ordinary Settlement. The people will stop working in the Ordinary Settlement. They will stop needing to eat. Our oxygen replaces any hunger as the person's body is changed to our requirements. There will be no need for any communication or individual thought. Any humanity will be removed. The Pure Human's skin will be cold and smooth and will glow, to be compatible with the materials they will eventually be changed into.'

'When they are ready, they will be told to come to the Pure Human City and after the final stage of the Organisation Reps scanning their hands to complete the conversion process, they will be ready to be used.'

Kyle stared at the page. His brain felt numb; he could barely breathe. The Organisation had thought of everything. Once a Pure Oxygen Machine was in a home in the Ordinary Settlement, the people were doomed. Nothing could save them.

His parents obviously knew something was wrong, Kyle thought. They were so adamant in their opposition to the Pure Oxygen Machines and had never allowed him near a home which had a Pure Oxygen Machine in it. He wondered what they would do if they knew exactly what the Organisation had planned.

Kyle read the next section, Organisation Reps.

'An Organisation Rep's job is to gain the trust of the people in the Ordinary Settlement. They have to place *"The Origins of Paradise"* in the Library. They must call the Ordinary Settlement an Ordinary Settlement until none of the people remember what the village was originally called.' Kyle had no idea that the Ordinary Settlement had ever had any other name.

'The Organisation Rep is responsible for placing a Pure Oxygen Machine in a house and for removing the Pure Oxygen Machine when the people are converted into Pure Humans.'

'The Organisation wants the people of the Ordinary Settlement to feel that the Ordinary Settlement is inferior to the Pure Human City. The Organisation Rep has to convince the people of the Ordinary Settlement that they need a Pure Oxygen Machine.'

'The Organisation Rep is the face of the Organisation. As well as working in the Ordinary Settlement, the Organisation Rep will work in the Pure Human City. They will be responsible for organising, controlling, and recycling the Pure Humans. The Organisation Rep will communicate through thought in the Pure Human City and through speech in the Ordinary Settlement.'

'Their last duty is to eliminate any intruders. The Organisation doesn't want any people in the Ordinary Settlement to know the truth of the Organisation's plans.'

Kyle felt a chill rush through him as he read the bit about eliminating intruders. He suddenly felt in extreme danger. *Should he close the book right now and leave?* He decided to read on. The more information he had, the more he could tell his parents. Pure Human City was the next section.

'The Pure Human City is our temporary home. We will mine the rocks/minerals we need using Pure Humans, and harvest the population of the Planet. The Pure Oxygen Machines will turn the people of the Ordinary Settlement into Pure Humans. Our mining and recycling operations are in the Pure Human City.'

'Currently 70% of the population has been converted, and they are working at maximum efficiency. More people of the Ordinary Settlement will be converted into Pure Humans until our mining operations have been completed. At this point, any remaining people will be rounded up and converted, so they can be recycled for future use.'

Kyle couldn't think anymore. His brain was struggling to cope, but he read on. Pure Oxygen Machines was the heading in the next section.

'Pure Oxygen Machines create air which contains special properties. The person breathing this air is converted from a human into a living robot – a Pure Human. Their body's structures are changed at the molecular level. The human cells will become building blocks for our building materials. The Pure Human will cease to think or act on their own, accepting instructions from the Organisation Reps. We will use the Pure Humans to build more buildings and to use in our future plans.'

Organisation Aims was the next section. 'We, as an Organisation, have come to this Planet to strip it of all the resources we need. Firstly the rocks/minerals, and secondly the population. The population converted into Pure Humans will mine the rocks/minerals and then be recycled when they are of no further use.'

'Our main aim is to split the population apart, making it easier to get the Pure Oxygen Machines into the Ordinary Settlement homes. Whatever we have to do, we will succeed. Eventually all the resources will be achieved. The rocks/minerals we mine will be converted to the materials we require for the next stage of our expansion.'

Kyle remembered to breathe. Thoughts tumbled through his brain. There was so much information to take in – Pure Humans, mining, rocks/minerals, recycling. *What on earth was going on? Where was this mine which the book referred to? How did the Organisation think they could get away with turning people from the Ordinary Settlement into Pure Humans just to become miners?*

Everyone was to be rounded up and converted. Then they would be recycled. *Why had no-one tried to stop the Organisation? What made the Organisation think they would be successful?*

His fingers found another page, but he had no time to read any further. He needed to tell his parents all of this right now. They had to listen. He needed to leave the Pure Human City now, before he was discovered.

He closed the book and placed it back on the desk, torn between reading further and getting out safely.

The doorway became visible as he approached the wall, and he placed his hand on the luminous circle. The door slid open. He moved slowly into the corridor, having listened carefully for any footsteps. He didn't see anyone. Taking a deep breath, he headed towards the stairs.

He paused before he turned into the landing to stand at the top of the stairs, and listened again. Silence. As quietly as he could, he headed down the stairs, treading carefully whilst trying to be as quick as possible. He made it to the first floor. He paused again. Nothing. He carried on to the entrance hall. He wanted to run, but knew he had to be careful. He wasn't out of the Pure Human City yet.

The distance between the bottom of the stairs and the open doorway seemed enormous. Glancing around, Kyle went for it.

He peered round one side of the open doorway, looking out onto the meeting place. It was empty. He spied the top of the road which he had come up to reach the meeting place. If he could get there, he could hide behind the buildings until he reached the place where the Pure Humans entered the Pure Human City.

What he was going to do when he got there he had no idea, but he would think of something. Telling himself he had to walk not run, he left the Organisation Headquarters. At each step he wanted to sprint away, but forced himself to be calm.

When he reached the first building, he ducked behind it and took a moment to get his breath. He couldn't believe he had ever thought the Pure Human City was a place he would want his parents to come to. *'The Origins of Paradise'* had painted a very different picture of life there. When Kyle looked at the building he was behind now, all he could think of was Pure Humans being recycled somehow. He shivered. Sweat trickled down his back.

He quickly made his way to the place where he had entered the Pure Human City. The forcefield was completely solid, but he had to get out.

He peered cautiously out from the back of the building. Someone would have to come or go sometime, wouldn't they?

Kyle waited for what seemed like hours. Just when he was giving up on ever escaping, the forcefield opened to reveal the woods. A group of Pure Humans entered. Kyle quickly dived behind them and ran out into the clearing.

He moved away from the gap in the forcefield, going right, so that he couldn't be spotted from inside the Pure Human City. His heart felt like it was going to explode. When the gap closed, he would run through the woods to the Ordinary Settlement and the safety of his parents.

He was just about to creep back to see if the gap had closed when he heard voices. He froze. The voices had to be Organisation Reps; the Pure Humans never spoke.

The Organisation Reps were laughing. It sounded odd to Kyle after being in the silence of the Pure Human City for so long. His breathing seemed too loud in his ears. He listened harder.

The two were discussing talking rather than communicating by thought. They both agreed thought was much better. One announced he had to go to the Ordinary Settlement. The other commiserated, saying that at least it wouldn't be long and then they'd be able to communicate how they liked. The first agreed happily.

Kyle crept closer to the gap and saw an Organisation Rep walking away from the forcefield towards the woods. It looked like the Organisation Rep Kyle had seen in the Ordinary Settlement.

The Organisation Rep never looked back. Kyle looked at the forcefield. The gap had closed up. He watched until the Organisation Rep had gone into the woods, and waited enough time for the Organisation Rep to get to the Ordinary Settlement.

Then Kyle dashed into the woods. He ran as fast as he could. There was no time to lose.

Chapter 7

It didn't take him long to return to the Ordinary Settlement, as he ran the whole way. When he burst through the front door, his parents were home and they looked furious.

Before he could open his mouth, they demanded to know where he had been. They had been looking for him after their meeting had finished, and had been told he had been spotted going into the woods.

Kyle stared at his parents in the growing silence; a silence much worse than that in the Pure Human City.

The question of who had spotted him going into the woods briefly passed through his brain, but he didn't follow up this thought. He was too scared of his parents. He had never seen them this angry before.

Words jumbled in his head. He had to tell them about 'The Origins of Paradise', about the Pure Human City, about the 'Operation Manual' and about the Pure Humans. But he just didn't know where to start. His parents still hadn't said a word.

He took a deep breath and started hesitantly, saying he had something to tell them about the Pure Human City. Something he thought they needed to know.

He never got any further. He was interrupted by his mum, who said she had something to tell him, too. It had been decided at the Ordinary Settlement meeting that he was old enough to be told all about the Organisation, the Pure Oxygen Machines, and the Pure Human City. Information he had been asking about for a long time.

Kyle was stunned; he hadn't expected this. His mum went on to say that she didn't know whether to tell him now or not, as he clearly had learned some information about the Pure Human City all by himself, although she wasn't sure how he'd done this.

Before he could stop himself, he blurted out that he had been into the Pure Human City. He carried on, saying he had been to the Library and read 'The Origins of Paradise', he'd read the 'Operations Manual' in the Organisation Headquarters, and had seen Pure Humans. He had to tell them everything he had seen and read; it was really important.

His father exploded, demanding to know why Kyle couldn't do as he was told. Why had Kyle to go and find out about matters he didn't need to know about?

Kyle tried to interrupt, but his dad cut him off and told Kyle to listen. Kyle didn't dare do anything else.

His dad told Kyle all about how the Organisation had come to the village, immediately building their Office and telling everyone about their wonderful

Pure Oxygen Machines. His dad had watched people from the village – called the Ordinary Settlement by the Organisation – turning from humans into something else. These people no longer worked in the village or participated in any way in village life. Then they went to the Pure Human City, never to be seen or heard from again.

A group of adults had decided the Organisation wasn't to be trusted. So they had kept the children away from the Library in the hope that they could protect them from reading and believing the lies in 'The Origins of Paradise'. The adults didn't believe what 'The Origins of Paradise' said.

Kyle was surprised. His dad clearly knew about 'The Origins of Paradise' when Kyle had thought he was the only one who knew about it. Kyle asked his dad when he had read 'The Origins of Paradise'. His dad stared at him for a moment; silence developed again as Kyle stood nervously waiting for a response.

His dad eventually replied that it didn't matter when he had read 'The Origins of Paradise'. All that mattered, he said, was that Kyle was kept away from the Organisation and the Pure Oxygen Machines.

Desperately, Kyle tried to tell his parents that they were in danger, that they had to hear what he had to say. It didn't matter how angry his parents were with him. They had to know the truth.

But each time he tried to say something, his parents cut him off, telling him they didn't want to know. The less they knew the better, they said. Once the Organisation had gone, everything would go back to normal. Yet Kyle knew that this was never going to happen.

His dad finally snapped, telling Kyle to keep his information to himself and not to scare any of the other children. As he left the house with Kyle's mum, his dad added that no-one would stop Kyle seeing what happened when a Pure Oxygen Machine went into a house. Kyle was free to go anywhere in the Ordinary Settlement now. There were tears in his mum's eyes as she was led out of the house by her husband.

Kyle stared in disbelief as his parents left. He hadn't expected anything like that to happen. Unsure of what to do next, he paced slowly round the room. He had to find a way to get them to listen to him.

What information would make his parents listen? What information would they like to know? His mind whizzed through everything he knew: Pure Humans, the Organisation plans, the Pure Human City, Pure Oxygen Machines. That was it – Pure Oxygen Machines.

He would go back to the Pure Human City and into the Organisation Headquarters. When he was there previously, he hadn't read one of the pages in the *'Operations Manual'*. It might contain information on how to stop a Pure Oxygen Machine working. It was worth checking.

Without another thought, he left the house at a run, heading towards the woods and the Pure Human City.

Chapter 8

He had a clear plan of what he was going to do when he got into the Pure Human City. He would head straight to the Organisation Headquarters and to the office on the second floor. Kyle felt very confident as the woods flew past. Before he knew it, he was at the edge of the clearing again.

He waited until a group of Pure Humans gathered in front of the forcefield, then hid among them. This time he was calm and thinking clearly.

It struck him that there were more Pure Humans in this group than the previous one he had followed into the Pure Human City, but he put that down to more people being converted on this occasion. He focussed on the forcefield and the moment when he could slip away from the Pure Humans, once the group had entered the Pure Human City.

He didn't have to wait long. The gap appeared in the forcefield and the group moved in. Spotting several Organisation Reps approaching the Pure Humans – boxes in hands – he slid away from the group of Pure

Humans and hid behind the nearest building. It was the one where he had hidden before.

So far so good, he thought. Peeking round the corner to check he hadn't been seen, Kyle pulled his head back quickly. An Organisation Rep had been looking directly in his direction. He didn't want to be caught and eliminated, as the *'Operations Manual'* had implied intruders would be.

He hid behind the next building to be safe. Cautiously, he peered round towards where he had just been. An Organisation Rep was standing there, a thoughtful look on his face. Kyle jumped back, suddenly becoming aware of his breathing; it sounded awfully loud. He waited a moment then peered round the building again. The Organisation Rep was gone.

The question was, had the Organisation Rep returned to the Pure Humans, or was he still looking? Kyle needed to know the answer before he could go any further.

He had to think carefully about his next move.

Should he risk going round the building towards the road and possibly being seen by the Organisation Reps? Or should he carry on behind the buildings towards the meeting place, and risk being detected as he moved from building to building?

Frustrated, he weighed up each option. He needed to get to the Organisation Headquarters as soon as possible. He had no idea when the Organisation would reach the completion stage in its plans, and he couldn't risk being too late to save his parents. He took a deep breath and decided to move from building to building.

As he prepared to move to the next building, he wondered why the Organisation Rep had been looking in his direction. That worry would have to wait; right now what was important was getting to the Organisation Headquarters.

He sprinted between the buildings on the way to the meeting place, pausing each time to make sure no-one was around. By the time he was looking out onto the meeting place, he was quite breathless.

The sight before him stunned him. The meeting place was filled with Pure Humans; lots and lots of Pure Humans. More than when Kyle had been there previously. Around the Pure Humans were Organisation Reps. Their eyes occasionally glinted green as they looked over all the Pure Humans, who stood still with fixed smiles on their faces.

Kyle saw the Pure Humans he had come in with being led into the meeting place by the Organisation Reps. There seemed to be gaps in how the Pure Humans were standing. He wondered why. But how could he find out? More and more Pure Humans filled the meeting place.

A group formed near Kyle, and he dived between them, careful not to move them. He didn't want to alert the Organisation Reps to his presence.

At the edge of the gap he discovered a Pure Oxygen Machine, sitting in the middle of the open space.

The Pure Humans weren't being put into the buildings this time. Kyle wondered why. *What was happening? What had changed? Each gap had to contain a Pure Oxygen Machine.*

Kyle had expected this visit to be like his first. In his head, he had imagined easily entering the Organisation Headquarters. But there was no way that was going to happen. There were too many Pure Humans and Organisation Reps.

Something was happening that Kyle didn't know about. He remembered the Organisation's determination in the *'Operations Manual'* to keep what happened in the Pure Human City secret from the Ordinary Settlement. The Organisation Reps would be extra careful if they thought an intruder had come into the Pure Human City.

Kyle shivered. If there was no chance of getting into the Organisation Headquarters, his best plan was to leave the Pure Human City. He would have to find another way to persuade his parents to listen to him.

He began to make his way carefully through the Pure Humans, back to where he had come from, and was nearly there when – as one – the Pure Humans moved. Kyle had nowhere to go and he found himself being swept along.

Scared that the Organisation Reps would spot him, he tried to act like a Pure Human, smiling like them as best as he could.

Panic rose in Kyle. This wasn't what he had planned at all. He had no idea where he was going. His group of Pure Humans walked into the 'Work Place'. Kyle, helpless, had to go with them, passing the Organisation Headquarters, where he really wanted to be.

Chapter 9

Organisation Reps lined the entrance to the 'Work Place', so Kyle had to keep going. Further and further into the unknown he headed. He kept going until he was absolutely certain there were no Organisation Reps around, then stopped to see where he was.

He was totally lost. He had no idea where he was or how to get back to the entrance of the 'Work Place'. Around him the Pure Humans moved on down the wide tunnel. The walls were lined with the same material the buildings were made of, with light coming from them. All Kyle could imagine was lots and lots of Pure Humans, melted to create these walls. He needed to get out of here as soon as possible. It was too eerie for him.

He took a step sideways, heading up the way he had come – and fell into nothing. He tried to grab onto something to stop himself from falling, and caught the arm of a Pure Human. Kyle jumped to his feet, his hands slamming themselves to his sides, but the Pure Human carried on walking, as if Kyle wasn't there.

Kyle looked around. He was standing at the beginning of a smaller tunnel which led away to his right. The walls were lined like the wider tunnel and he couldn't see where it ended. Kyle stood trying to catch his breath and to understand exactly what was going on.

He peered into the wider tunnel and saw more tunnels, leading off the wider tunnel. The Pure Humans were going down them.

He was faced with a dilemma. *Did he go up the wider tunnel – the way he had come – and find the way out, or did he follow the Pure Humans down the smaller tunnel?*

He might meet an Organisation Rep if he went up the wider tunnel now. There had been a lot of Organisation Reps in the meeting place. If he waited, perhaps the Organisation Reps would be away from the meeting place when he returned there. He decided to follow the Pure Humans down the smaller tunnel.

Kyle tried to stay away from the tunnel walls and the Pure Humans. He hated the touch of the walls and the touch of the Pure Humans' skin. He longed to be in the Ordinary Settlement with its rundown brick buildings and real people. Never again would he complain of anything.

The tunnel went on for some distance, and after several turns Kyle had completely lost any sense of direction. He was beginning to wonder if the tunnel would ever end when he spotted an earth tunnel.

The Pure Humans around him walked into the earth tunnel. As they did, he saw the walls were narrower than the tunnel lined with the Pure Human

City building material. The Pure Humans glowed and gave off enough light for him to see clearly.

Kyle stared in shock and horror. Not only had the people of the Ordinary Settlement been dehumanised and totally changed, but they were being used as lights. He could only stare at the scene in front of him.

Some Pure Humans stood at regular intervals along the earth tunnel, providing the light. Evidently a Pure Human still needed light to see by. The rest of the Pure Humans went to the right earth tunnel wall and began to dig the earth with their hands, placing the earth on the stationary conveyor belt on the left hand side of the tunnel.

Kyle realised why there had been so many Pure Humans at the meeting place. They were needed if all the digging was done by hand.

Suddenly a realisation struck Kyle. This 'Work Place' was the mining which the *'Operations Manual'* had referred to. This work wasn't what had been promised by *'The Origins of Paradise'*. The Organisation had told so many lies.

Kyle was determined to get *'The Origins of Paradise'* out of the Library and destroy it. But he also needed to find out how to beat the Pure Oxygen Machines. This wasn't a fate he wanted for his parents. Getting to the Organisation Headquarters was his priority.

While he was thinking, Kyle had been staring at the Pure Humans who were digging. Something suddenly occurred to him; none of the earth stuck to the Pure Humans' hands.

He edged closer to the tunnel and put his hands in the earth. It clung to his hands, just like the earth in the fields in the Ordinary Settlement. He had to rub his hands together several times to get most of it off, eventually using the handkerchief in his pocket to remove the remnants. He shoved the earth-covered handkerchief back into his pocket.

The Pure Humans were either standing, acting as lights, or digging the earth; all had the same fixed smile on their faces. It was all too weird. It was time to leave.

The loud sound of a hiss had him staring down the earth tunnel, and he saw clouds of gas coming rapidly towards him. Kyle put his hand over his mouth to try and prevent breathing in the fumes which stuck in his throat. He coughed loudly. He tried to stop himself but he couldn't. He coughed again. An Organisation Rep was sure to hear him.

In desperation, he stumbled into the white-lined tunnel, slipping on the earth as he did so. His hands fell into the earth. He rubbed them against his clothes as he quickly moved into the white tunnel, away from the suffocating gas. He didn't stop until he could breathe normally and had stopped coughing.

Kyle leaned his back against the wall, calming his thoughts. Any moment now he was expecting to hear footsteps and see an Organisation Rep. He had nowhere to run to. He told himself to calm down. If he didn't, he was sure to be caught.

He looked at his hands and saw chunks of earth attached to them. Once again he used his handkerchief to clean his hands, so all the earth went into his pocket. If any earth was found in the white-lined tunnel, the Organisation Reps would definitely know a non-Pure Human was in the Pure Human City. The earth didn't stick to the Pure Humans' hands.

He turned to head up the white-lined tunnel, determined to find a way out of the 'Work Place' as soon as possible.

Something stopped him. He groaned. He had to know what had happened to the Pure Humans.

Cursing his curiosity, he cautiously headed back in the direction of the earth tunnel, listening all the time for the footsteps of an Organisation Rep.

When Kyle got back to the earth tunnel, the Pure Humans were all standing. They appeared unharmed. Kyle wondered what the point of the gas was; he couldn't think of any reason for it.

It became startlingly clear when he looked at the conveyor belt. Instead of earth, there were chunks of glowing silver. The conveyor belt began to move down into the earth tunnel.

Kyle could only stare. The more he learned, the more confusing it became. What could the Organisation want with the silver glowing chunks?

This was one question that would have to remain unanswered. He could hardly ask an Organisation Rep. If he did know the answer, it would probably mean he had been caught and was about to be changed into a Pure Human. If he was caught, he knew he would probably demand to know the answer, even if it wasn't going to be of any benefit to him. His demanding curiosity would see to that.

Finally happy that he had learned everything he could, Kyle turned away from the digging Pure Humans – the conveyor belt had come to a stop – and walked back up the white-lined tunnel.

After many turns, he reached the entrance to the side tunnel. Cautiously he peered into the wide tunnel. There was no-one about. Down every side tunnel he could see, he imagined lots of Pure Humans digging the earth, and shuddered. Taking a second look for safety, he slid into the wide tunnel and took a quick look up and down; he couldn't see where it began or ended. He began to head back the way he had come with the Pure Humans.

Kyle felt as though he had been walking up the tunnel forever. The whiteness of the walls never ceased. The silence was overwhelming. Kyle realised he had no idea of how much time he had been inside the Pure Human City.

He was about to give up when he saw the walls of the entrance to the 'Work Place'. His pulse quickened, and his footsteps got quicker. He couldn't wait to leave the Pure Human City, but first he had to get into the Organisation Headquarters. When he saw his parents next, he would promise never to disobey them again. His curiosity would never be allowed out again.

He slid up against the entrance wall, slowly looking round, just as an Organisation Rep came out of the Organisation Headquarters.

Kyle hurriedly pulled himself back behind the 'Work Place' entrance wall, praying he hadn't been seen. He dived down the nearest side tunnel.

Chapter 10

He had no idea if the Organisation Rep was coming into the 'Work Place'. All he knew was that he had to make certain he wasn't caught. He needed to see his parents again.

The pain in his side made him stop. He clutched his side, listening for footsteps between his noisy breaths. He was sure his breathing could be heard all the way along the tunnel.

He took several minutes to get himself together. He had been so close to the entrance and freedom. It seemed like he was never going to get out of the 'Work Place'. He was doomed to become a Pure Human – a disappointment in his parents' eyes. Kyle loved his parents and he needed them to know that.

He started to pay attention to his surroundings in a bid to take his mind off his parents.

He was at the end of the side tunnel. The earth tunnel was, he noticed, the same width as the white-lined tunnel. The Pure Humans, Kyle could see, were lining up against each side of the earth tunnel, and the conveyor belt was gone.

The Pure Humans stood with their backs to the earth tunnel walls, moving their arms from their sides so that their hands touched each other. The Pure Humans nearest to the white lining placed their hands on the white walls.

Kyle cried out as the white walls expanded down the earth tunnel, and the Pure Humans melted into them. He clamped his hand over his mouth. In a matter of seconds all the Pure Humans were engulfed. Kyle was left alone.

Determined, he turned away from the now longer side white tunnel. He was going to leave the 'Work Place', no matter what. He was going to leave the Pure Human City; the Organisation Headquarters could wait. All he had to do was convince his parents to leave the Ordinary Settlement so that they could be safe from the Organisation. Somehow he would do that, no matter what it took.

It took longer to get to the side tunnel entrance than Kyle remembered. Extremely carefully, he stuck his head round the entrance, scared he would be looking straight into the face of an Organisation Rep. But he wasn't. Instead, he was looking at the backs of several Organisation Reps who were standing in the 'Work Place' entrance, looking out onto the meeting place.

There was no way he was going to be able to get past them. *Was this the end for him? Were his parents and all the other people in the Ordinary Settlement destined to become Pure Humans, to be used as pawns by the Organisation?*

Kyle felt despair rising inside him. He had discovered so much, just to be stopped by the lack of an escape route. He wondered if he should just approach the Organisation Reps to get it over with quickly.

Movement caught his eye. Looking to his left, he saw some Pure Humans coming up the wide tunnel towards the 'Work Place' entrance. Kyle expected them to walk towards the Organisation Reps but they didn't. They headed through a tunnel on the extreme left of Kyle. He wouldn't have spotted it if the Pure Humans hadn't been going down it.

Kyle followed the Pure Humans as quickly and quietly as he could, checking that the Organisation Reps hadn't seen him. They hadn't. Kyle followed the Pure Humans at a slight distance, ready if he needed to hide from any Organisation Reps.

The Pure Humans walked into an empty open room, lined with the white building material. Kyle ducked behind a low wall between the tunnel and the room. He didn't know why it was there and didn't care. From the wall, he could see everything that was going on and possibly find his way out.

The Pure Humans went into the middle of the room and stopped. Kyle took a good look at them. Their faces weren't quite right. One side of their faces was crooked, the fixed smile drooping to one side. Their hands were misshapen, the fingers overlong or missing sections.

These Pure Humans obviously weren't suitable to become walls.

He was about to sneak out from behind the wall to see more of the room when more Pure Humans entered from the right. This meant there had to be a way in. A way in, which Kyle could use to leave.

Two Organisation Reps followed the Pure Humans. They were smiling broadly, and Kyle wondered what was amusing them. He soon found out.

One Pure Human – pushed by an Organisation Rep – collapsed to the floor, his leg giving way. Another Organisation Rep immediately lay down on the floor and changed into an exact copy of the fallen Pure Human. Kyle's hand was clamped over his mouth to stop his cry of astonishment.

The Organisation Rep who was standing, laughed out loud. The sound was unnatural in the silence of the Pure Human City. The Organisation Rep on the floor changed back to the way he had been before, and got to his feet.

Kyle could hardly believe what he had just seen. How could he possibly know who was who now? Everything had just got more complicated.

The Pure Humans had come to a halt and they stood around waiting. The two Organisation Reps lifted the Pure Human off the floor, shoving him between two Pure Humans who obligingly held him in their arms.

The Pure Humans moved until they were lined up in rows in front of the wall Kyle could see in front of him. He had a horrible feeling he knew what was about to happen. He was right.

The Pure Humans at the head of each line stepped forward and walked into the wall. Kyle didn't even want to cry out. It was sickening to see.

He watched as all the Pure Humans willingly became one with the wall. He couldn't look away. The Organisation Reps watched gleefully, occasionally laughing silently. It was extremely spooky.

Eventually there were no Pure Humans left. The two Organisation Reps left the room the way they had come in, and Kyle was left staring at an empty room. The silence was louder that it had been before. He felt totally and utterly alone, and helpless.

His parents wouldn't listen to anything he had to say. He wanted to save them from the fate he saw coming to them, but didn't know how. He shook himself out of his thoughts, then slid round the wall into the room, turning right. He desperately hoped he would see the exit and not the Organisation Reps.

Chapter 11

He was the only one in the room. Sighing with relief, he looked around. He saw solid white walls and tried not to think about the Pure Humans who made up the walls. To his right he saw the opening he needed.

Without any further thought, he sprang forward to the opening and peered out. He could see the meeting place. He could leave the Pure Human City after all.

Kyle almost ran out into the meeting place without checking for any Organisation Reps, but stopped himself just in time. It wouldn't do to get caught when he was so close to finding his way out.

The meeting place was empty of any Organisation Reps, but the Pure Oxygen Machines were still there. Kyle wondered how many more Pure Humans were still to come to the Pure Human City.

He saw the opening to the 'Work Place' and the Organisation Headquarters. That meant he must be in the 'Recreation Centre', where the Pure Humans were turned into the white building material. Now all he had to do was get to the Pure Human City entrance.

He stepped out into the meeting place and was half-way to the nearest road when he stopped. The Pure Humans were turned into the white building material. They were being recycled, just as the *'Operations Manual'* had described. Not as *'The Origins of Paradise'* had described the 'Recreation Centre'.

Kyle had seen and read so much that that he didn't think anything else could shock him. People from the Ordinary Settlement really believed everything they read in *'The Origins of Paradise'*, and the Organisation had dressed their lies up extremely well.

He stood in the meeting place for several minutes, unable to think or move. Slowly he realised where he was and fled to the top of one of the roads leading between the Pure Human City entrance and the meeting place.

He hid behind one of the single-storey buildings, wondering what had possessed him to stop for so long in the meeting place. *Did he want to get caught?* Shaking his head to clear it, he started back towards the Pure Human City entrance, ducking behind each building as he did so.

Sweat trickled down his back as he wondered how he was going to get out of the Pure Human City this time. The Organisation Reps might be looking for him if they thought there was an intruder in the Pure Human City. The Organisation Rep had been looking exactly where he had been hiding when he came in. That had been a close call, Kyle remembered.

From behind the back of a building, he watched two Organisation Reps as they stood where the entrance would be. To his surprise, they were talking aloud and laughing. He listened intently.

They were discussing the Organisation's plans. Kyle learned that the Organisation was almost at the final stage. The Pure Humans were mining the last of the rocks/minerals that were going to be needed. That explained why there were so many Pure Humans coming into the Pure Human City, Kyle realised, and why the Organisation Rep had been looking at where Kyle had hidden behind the building. Intruders were to be eliminated.

One Organisation Rep asked the other if the intruder had been caught yet. Kyle held his breath. He must have been spotted! The other Organisation Rep replied that the intruder had been spotted going into the mines and guided to the recycling centre, but had disappeared from that point.

So that was why the Organisation Reps had their backs to me at the 'Work Place' entrance, Kyle thought. They had forced him to go the 'Recreation Centre'. *What would they have done if they had caught him? Would he have been forced into the wall?* He stopped this train of thought; it was too horrible to contemplate.

He carried on listening to the Organisation Reps. They were agreeing that the intruder wouldn't go far, as there was nowhere to go. Both Organisation Reps laughed at this. 'And to think,' one Organisation Rep said, 'all the time the intruder is here, he's breathing Pure Oxygen. He's changing into a Pure Human without any need for us to do anything.'

Kyle froze. The Organisation Reps were right. He was becoming what he was most afraid of. He looked at his skin. There was a faint glow. He touched his arm. It was cooler than normal. He wasn't very hungry but he should be, as he had come straight back to the Pure Human City from his house after talking to his parents. This wasn't how it was meant to end.

He listened again to the Organisation Reps, numbness creeping through him. One Organisation Rep was thanking the other for practice in talking out loud. The other Organisation Rep said it was his pleasure; talking out loud meant more Pure Humans and more rocks/minerals for the Organisation.

The first Organisation Rep laughed and said he was going to the Ordinary Settlement to make some more Pure Humans. The people had promised to work hard, and had even asked for two Pure Oxygen Machines to speed up the process.

The second Organisation Rep laughed and wished the first Organisation Rep well. The first Organisation Rep thanked him and walked out through the entrance that had just appeared in the forcefield.

The second Organisation Rep was watching the group of Pure Humans who were now coming into the Pure Human City.

Kyle took his chance and slipped out of the entrance behind the second Organisation Rep's back.

The first Organisation Rep was walking towards the woods. Kyle ran to his left, around the forcefield, only stopping when he reached the woods. He hid behind a tree to catch his breath, swearing never to go into the Pure Human City again, and wondering who in the Ordinary Settlement wanted two Pure Oxygen Machines.

Chapter 12

He couldn't get to the Ordinary Settlement quick enough. He had to stop whoever wanted these two Pure Oxygen machines, and to talk to his parents. The wood passed in a blur.

He arrived at the Ordinary Settlement in time to see his friend, Freya, and her family happily following an Organisation Rep into their house. Freya waved and smiled at him when she saw him.

He was gathering his breath to warn her when he caught his dad looking at him. The shake of his father's head warned him to keep quiet. Kyle noticed other adults silently watching what was happening. His warning died in his throat.

The Organisation Rep came out of Freya's house. A forcefield, just like the one over the Pure Human City, went over Freya's house. Kyle knew it was too late. Freya and her family were beyond saving.

The watching adults exchanged sad looks and walked away from Freya's house. Kyle ran up to his parents, intending to try and talk to them, but the stern, forbidding look on his dad's face stopped him. His mum's eyes filled with tears as she and his father walked away. Kyle was left alone with the shimmering forcefield around Freya's house.

It was hopeless. There was no way his parents were going to listen to him. He found the nearest building and sat on the ground, his back against the building wall, regardless of the mud on the ground.

What was he going to do? The only option left was to go back to the Pure Human City and find out how to disable the Pure Oxygen machines.

He didn't want to go back. Apart from the risk of getting caught, he would be exposed to more Pure Oxygen. He wanted to remain who he was.

Unable to think of anything else, he headed to his house, hoping his parents would let him in. The house was empty when he reached it; his parents must be in the fields.

In the kitchen he found a plate of food with a note beside it. The note, from his mum, said that she loved him and hoped he would stop talking about the Pure Human City, so that his dad would talk to him.

Kyle ate the food, determined to be human. He wasn't sure if he tasted it or not, but he made sure he finished all of it.

He sat staring into space for a while, not sure how to proceed. In the end, he wrote a note to his parents, explaining everything he had learned. His mum would read it even if his dad wouldn't.

He wasn't tired, so he left the house and found somewhere to sit and watch Freya's house. He didn't know what good it would do, but he couldn't think of anything else to do. He doubted if his parents would want him to be with them in the fields.

His mind ran over everything he knew. He watched the Organisation Rep come and go from Freya's house, presumably to check on the Pure Humans' progress. He was in a state of limbo.

He wasn't sure how much time had passed. No-one in the Ordinary Settlement came near Freya's house. Kyle occasionally heard children's voices, and adults turning the children away from where Freya's house was.

Kyle felt so alone. He wished he was one of the children being turned away, ignorant of any of the Organisation's plans. He wished he had never read 'The Origins of Paradise'.

He jerked out of his stupor. Of course, 'The Origins of Paradise'. He raced to the Library. As he approached, Freya was leaving the Library with a book under her arm and walked past, not seeing him at all. Kyle wondered when she had left her house. He had been watching very closely.

He flung open the Library door, not waiting to see if anyone was inside, and headed straight to the table where he had last seen 'The Origins of Paradise'. It was gone!

Kyle tossed the books off the table searching for 'The Origins of Paradise', but found nothing. Frantically, he searched all the tables in the Library and every single reading room, just in case someone had come in and moved 'The Origins of Paradise'.

Freya must have it! This meant only one thing: the Organisation was ready for the final stage of its plans.

He left the Library, books strewn everywhere, making no attempt to clear up. He went back to Freya's house to see what was going to happen next.

The Organisation Rep kept coming and going, looking happier each time he left Freya's house. Kyle was worried. A happy Organisation Rep meant trouble.

He was watching at some point – Kyle didn't know when, because he had no idea of how much time had passed – when he saw the usual Organisation Rep go into Freya's house with two other Organisation Reps.

Suddenly the forcefield fell away from the house. Freya and her family followed the usual Organisation Rep and headed out of the Ordinary Settlement. Freya was carrying 'The Origins of Paradise'. The other two Organisation Reps walked in the opposite direction, carrying the two Pure Oxygen Machines. *They must be going to the Office of the Organisation*, Kyle thought.

Kyle followed Freya, her family, and the Organisation Rep, fully aware of where they were going. He decided to follow them until they got to the clearing and then… Well, he wasn't sure what. He would have to decide what to do when he got there.

He alternately walked openly behind the group or moved behind the houses, depending on how many people were about. Not many people were left in the

Ordinary Settlement now, and many of those worked in the fields all day to ensure that there was food to eat. The mud helped to hide his footsteps.

Several times the Organisation Rep looked around, and Kyle hid as best as he could. He just hoped he hadn't been spotted. He thought he saw the Organisation Rep giving a small smile, but wasn't sure. Uneasiness grew in him.

Freya and her family obediently followed the Organisation Rep. Kyle felt sick knowing exactly what was waiting for Freya and her family at the Pure Human City.

When the Organisation Rep reached the woods, Kyle hung back to let the group get ahead of him. It would be difficult to hide his footsteps in the wood. He waited for a short while then headed off at a run in a slightly different direction, which would take him to the clearing.

Kyle stopped at the clearing edge and saw Freya and her family join more Pure Humans waiting to get into the Pure Human City. The Organisation Rep stood by the forcefield.

The fixed smiles on Freya and her family's faces were horrible to see. Kyle tried to remember the smile Freya had given him when he had returned to the Ordinary Settlement. He couldn't. All he could see was the Pure Human fixed smile.

What should he do? Turn and go back to the Ordinary Settlement, or go once more into the Pure Human City? Either way I'm doomed, he thought.

If he went back to the Ordinary Settlement, he would be rounded up and taken to the Pure Human City. He was sure his parents wouldn't be able to stop this happening. He could hide and probably escape capture, but then he'd be alone.

If he went to the Pure Human City, he would be breathing more Pure Oxygen. He desperately wanted his last remnants of human to remain. Kyle couldn't foresee a good ending.

He decided. He would go into the Pure Human City, knowing there was a chance he would be turned into a Pure Human and never leave. He had to try to find out how to disable the Pure Oxygen Machines to save his parents.

Once again he joined the group of Pure Humans waiting to get into the Pure Human City, making sure the Organisation Rep didn't see him. He edged close to Freya, planning to grab *'The Origins of Paradise'* from her when the Organisation Rep was concentrating on getting the Pure Humans into the Pure Human City.

Chapter 13

His chance never came. For whatever reason, Freya moved up to the Organisation Rep when the forcefield parted. Kyle didn't dare get that close to the Organisation Rep, so he had to watch, agonised, as Freya followed the Organisation Rep into the Pure Human City. Kyle wondered if she was deliberately being kept by the Organisation Rep's side because she had 'The Origins of Paradise'.

Abandoning his plan to get hold of 'The Origins of Paradise', he decided to concentrate instead on getting to the Organisation Headquarters and finding the 'Operations Manual' again. This was his last chance to save his parents and the rest of the people from the Ordinary Settlement. He needed to read the one page he hadn't read.

He dived behind the nearest building as soon as he entered the Pure Human City, then kept going. He didn't stop to watch the Organisation Reps scanning the new Pure Humans' hands.

As quickly as he could, he got to the meeting place. It was empty. Kyle took a breath of courage and determination, and ran to the Organisation Headquarters entrance. He flung his back against the wall just inside the entrance, took one more breath, then ran to the stairs.

He flew up the stairs to the second floor, headed to the left, and looked for the office he had been in before. The door was open.

Sliding in, he checked he was alone. He was. He suddenly realised he hadn't done a lot of checking for any Organisation Reps, as he had been so intent on getting to the office to find the 'Operations Manual'.

He closed the office door and turned his attention to the desk. The 'Operations Manual' was still there. He crouched behind the desk and turned to the last page.

It was headed up, 'Warning'. Kyle's heart lightened a little, hoping this was good news for him. 'Warning,' he read. 'At no time should the Pure Oxygen Machine touch the Planet surface. Always ensure the pedestal is between the ground and the Pure Oxygen Machine. Any contact will decrease the efficiency of the Pure Oxygen Machine.'

Kyle stared at the page. The answer seemed so simple; get the Pure Oxygen Machine to touch the earth! *But how was he going to do that in the Pure Human City, when all the buildings and roads were made of the special building material?* The earth in the mines or 'Work Place' was too far away.

His spark of hope faded. It was useless; he couldn't save anyone.

Tears began to fill his eyes. He pushed his hand into his pocket to get his handkerchief, and felt the earth lying at the bottom of his pocket. *He did have something he could use!*

He ran the backs of his hands over his eyes, wiping away his tears. If he could throw the earth over a Pure Oxygen Machine, maybe it would stop it working properly. A new feeling of hope sparked inside him. This was what he needed to know.

Even if he disrupted only a few Pure Oxygen Machines, it would enable some people to fight back. The Organisation wouldn't win. He gazed triumphantly at the *'Operations Manual'*. He had won the battle.

Suddenly a shadow stopped his thoughts in their tracks. He looked up. Standing above him was the Organisation Rep who had led Freya and her family to their house. There was a dangerous smile on the Organisation Rep's face, and green triumph flashed in his eyes.

Hands grabbed Kyle from behind, yanking him to his feet. Without any words, he was propelled to the office door. The Ordinary Settlement Organisation Rep opened it and Kyle was bodily moved down the corridor towards the dead end. Kyle knew a room was there. Still the Organisation Rep said nothing.

Eventually the Organisation Rep turned to Kyle and smiled. 'Ready?' Kyle heard in his head. Kyle flinched. The Organisation Rep's smile broadened. Kyle had heard the Organisation Rep. *He was losing his humanness and had no idea how to hang onto it.* The Organisation Rep turned to the dead end and opened the door. Kyle was taken inside.

He stood in the middle of the room, his arms held in a vice-tight grip. He couldn't have moved if he had wanted to. He was so scared. This was his worst nightmare come true. Any moment now he would be pushed into the walls and swallowed up. He would be powerless to stop it happening.

He had heard the Organisation Rep in his head, so he must be a Pure Human. The wall would take him, just like it had taken all the other Pure Humans. Kyle had no idea if there was anything else in the room; all he was focusing on was the Organisation Rep.

The Organisation Rep faced him, an evil smile on his face. Silence stretched into the room. Kyle thought he was going to burst. Still the Organisation Rep was silent.

Kyle tried to escape his captors, struggling against their hold but their grip only got tighter. Pain ran through his arms. *He was still partly an alive human!* Hope soared in his heart. He had felt the pain. He could still make a difference. He struggled harder.

'Enough!' shouted through his head. He stopped in shock. The Organisation Rep had talked to him again in his head. The Organisation Rep smiled a satisfied smile and carried on talking in his head.

'Now I have your attention, let me say how pleased we are to see you. You had us puzzled for a while. Someone had got into the Pure Human City who wasn't a Pure Human. We had no idea how you had done this, and really wanted to meet you to ask you how you got in.' Kyle didn't respond.

The Organisation Rep continued.

'We don't get many people surviving exposure to Pure Oxygen and lasting as long as you have. Normally the intruders are caught quickly.'

So there had been others, Kyle thought, surprised that he wasn't the first.

'Yes, there have been,' he heard in reply to his thought. Kyle froze. He couldn't even think now!

The Organisation Rep continued. 'You were followed once you were in the Pure Human City, and allowed to get to the Organisation Headquarters. We wanted to see what you would do. Well done in finding the office and our *'Operations Manual'*. We hope you found it interesting.' Kyle realised now that the Organisation had been playing with him.

The Organisation Rep went on. 'You spent a long time watching our newest recruits in the Ordinary Settlement.' *Freya*, Kyle thought involuntarily.

'Freya,' Kyle heard. 'What a lovely name. She was very useful in getting you to come into the Pure Human City. Did you like the way she moved up to me when all the new Pure Humans came into the Pure Human City? We wanted to be sure you would come and join us.' The Organisation Rep paused briefly, and then carried on. 'I enjoyed watching you follow Freya through the Ordinary Settlement. You are a true friend.'

Kyle was beginning to get angry. The Organisation Rep was talking about Freya as if she was bait. No-one talked about his friend like that and got away with it.

Kyle had never considered that the Organisation Rep might have been watching him in the Ordinary Settlement. Kyle had thought he would be safe there.

Again the Organisation Rep interrupted his thoughts.

'You had to be the intruder. You spent too long watching Freya's house.' Kyle was going to shout, he could feel it coming but the Organisation Rep carried on talking.

'No person from the Ordinary Settlement could have stayed awake as long as you did. Thank you for helping us identify you.'

Kyle had had enough. He shouted angrily at the Organisation Rep, determined to let him know the Organisation weren't going to have things all their own way.

He told the Organisation Rep about his first visit to the Pure Human City and how he had realised the truth, that what was said in *'The Origins of Paradise'* was a lie.

He said he had read the *'Operations Manual'* and knew everything the Organisation had planned for the people of the Ordinary Settlement and the Planet's rocks/minerals. He explained that he knew what really went on at the 'Work Place' and the 'Recreation Centre', and described seeing the earth turn into silver glowing chunks.

He said he knew how to stop the Pure Oxygen Machines working properly and finished by saying he had told his parents everything. He wasn't the only one who knew the Organisation's plans.

The Organisation Rep shook his head sadly. 'Please think,' Kyle heard the Organisation Rep say. 'It's much more civilised. Talking out loud is so outdated.'

Kyle screamed in rage. The sound echoed off the walls. Eventually silence returned to the room.

He heard the Organisation Rep again. 'You have been very busy. You have learned more than other people. We congratulate you. However, whatever you or your parents know will make no difference. We always succeed.'

Kyle struggled again to break the hold on his arms. He wanted to launch himself at the Organisation Rep, but his efforts only yielded pain.

He heard the Organisation Rep again. 'It won't do any good struggling, you know. We always catch any intruders and dispose of them.'

Kyle was still. *What was his fate to be?*

'Sometimes,' Kyle heard, 'we allow them to walk into the wall at the Recycling Centre, regardless of their stage of conversion.' Kyle shivered. He couldn't see that as an attractive option.

'Sometimes,' Kyle heard, 'we allow them to become Pure Humans, using the box to scan their hand.' Kyle didn't like this option either. He wanted to remain a human.

'And sometimes,' Kyle heard, 'we let them turn into a Pure Human naturally.'

Kyle stared in amazement at the Organisation Rep. He had always thought the Pure Humans had to have their hands scanned to complete the conversion process. That was what he had read in the 'Operations Manual'.

The Organisation Rep answered his thoughts. 'The box, as you have so rightly thought, is used to complete the conversion process. It is used to get the Pure Humans working quickly.'

'Which option do you think you would like?'

Kyle had no answer. He just wanted to be in the Ordinary Settlement with his parents.

The Organisation Rep paused for a moment then moved a little closer to Kyle. 'With you, we are going to let you change naturally. We want you to have the hope of remaining human whilst knowing your humanity is draining away.' The Organisation Rep leaned closer again to Kyle. 'You will turn into a Pure Human.'

The Organisation Rep gave Kyle a look of excited anticipation and carried on. 'The last moments are always the best, seeing the person struggle to hold onto their humanity.'

If Kyle had been alone, he would have cried. It was so unfair. All he had wanted to do was protect his parents and the people of the Ordinary Settlement. First it had been his parents and their beliefs, and now the Organisation was getting in his way. He swallowed his bubbling emotions and looked defiantly at the Organisation Rep.

The Organisation Rep continued, 'Before you join us, let's go and see everyone from the Ordinary Settlement. You can say your goodbyes before you fully join us.' Kyle was turned around and marched out of the room after the Organisation Rep, who had opened the door.

He suddenly remembered the silver glowing chunks. Kyle had to know what they were for. Before he could stop himself, he demanded – out loud – to know what they were for. His curiosity was too strong to be denied.

The Organisation Rep turned to face Kyle, and he was brought to a halt. 'Ah yes. The silver glowing chunks are being used to enable the Organisation to complete a special project. So special, in fact, that it isn't in the *'Operations Manual'*. You did well seeing them. Not many people do.'

The Organisation Rep turned away from Kyle again and walked along the corridor. Kyle was pushed into following the Organisation Rep. He knew what he was about to see.

Chapter 14

He was brought to a halt outside the Organisation Headquarters. There in front of him were all the remaining people from the Ordinary Settlement, surrounded by Pure Humans. Kyle saw his parents holding each other. Other adults were holding their children close to them or clinging to each other. Fear was clearly visible on all their faces. The children's frightened cries filled the meeting place.

The Pure Humans formed an impenetrable barrier around them. Pure Oxygen Machines formed another barrier between the people of the Ordinary Settlement and the Pure Humans, including Freya and her family. Kyle tried to count them but there were too many. The Organisation was taking no chances, aiming to get the job done quickly. Kyle fought against his captors again, but was still held tight.

He saw other Organisation Reps standing around the meeting place, ensuring that if any person from the Ordinary Settlement got out of the circle they would have no chance of escaping.

Kyle saw his parents catch sight of him. They looked afraid. Kyle wished they had listened to him. His mum's eyes filled with tears when she saw him. His dad bowed his head.

'Watch and learn,' Kyle heard inside his head. 'This will soon be you.' Kyle turned his head and stared at the Organisation Rep, who smiled a satisfied smile. Kyle quickly turned his gaze back to the group of people from the Ordinary Settlement. He was determined not to show any emotion. He didn't want to give the Organisation Rep any satisfaction.

Inside he was in turmoil. He could see no way to help anyone. It didn't seem he could even help himself. All his plans to stop the Pure Oxygen Machines had come to nothing. It seemed that the Organisation was going to win, after all.

Kyle watched as one by one the people of the Ordinary Settlement succumbed to the conversion process. Parents stopped holding their children. Children no longer made any noise. Silence fell over the meeting place. Kyle saw his parents let go of each other and stare ahead. The eerie smiles began to appear on the people's faces. Kyle felt himself die inside; his connection with his parents was draining away.

The Pure Humans who were surrounding the people from the Ordinary Settlement stepped back. *It must mean the Organisation was close to winning,* Kyle thought. *No person from the Ordinary Settlement would give them any trouble now.*

The Organisation Reps from around the meeting place began to remove some of the Pure Oxygen Machines, leaving a gap in the circle.

Kyle screamed, the sound filling the meeting place. He struggled against the hands holding him, pleased to feel pain as they tightened their grip on his arms. There was still something of him left. *If he could get to the remaining Pure Oxygen Machines, maybe he could stop some of them working. But how?*

The Organisation Rep stepped forward, and Kyle saw Freya coming towards him with 'The Origins of Paradise' in her hands.

Kyle stood as still as he could, hoping the Organisation Reps holding him would think he was finally coming to the end of the conversion process and loosen their grip on his arms. He felt the pressure on his arms lighten.

Carefully, Kyle watched Freya. She offered 'The Origins of Paradise' to the Organisation Rep, who took it with a triumphant smile.

As he accepted the book, Kyle suddenly pulled away from his captors and ran to the people of the Ordinary Settlement. He heard voices shouting in his head, 'Catch him!'

He put his hand into his pocket, grabbed the dirt, and flung it over the Pure Oxygen Machines nearest to his parents. He thought he saw a flicker across his dad's face, but didn't get a chance to watch further as hands grabbed his arms and spun him around to face the Organisation Rep. He looked angry, and then amused.

'We'll put you somewhere where you can't interfere,' Kyle heard. 'Relish your last moments, they're coming soon.'

Kyle was afraid. *Why*, he wondered, *was it taking so long for him to convert when the people from the Ordinary Settlement had converted so quickly?*

The Organisation Rep answered his thought. 'The harder you fight, the longer it takes to convert. Please fight hard, I want you to suffer.'

Kyle was marched towards the entrance of the Organisation Headquarters. He briefly managed to twist round and glimpsed the people from the Ordinary Settlement being led to the 'Recreation Centre', his mum and dad leading the way.

Inside the Organisation Headquarters he was led halfway along the left hand wall of the hall. The Organisation Rep placed his right hand on the wall and the familiar circle appeared. The door to a room slid back and Kyle was pushed inside.

He stumbled forward, then turned round as quickly as he could and saw the door closing. Frantically he pressed his hands over the wall, trying to find the circle to open the door. He couldn't find it. He searched for several minutes and eventually stood defeated in the middle of the room. There had to be some locking mechanism he didn't know about.

He was going to turn into a Pure Human. He just had to wait for it to happen.

Kyle sat on the floor his back against a wall, resigned to his fate, quickly jumping to his feet when he felt himself beginning to sink into the wall. He wasn't ready to be swallowed up just yet. He moved to sit in the middle of the room, well away from any of the walls.

Jumbled thoughts ran through his head. *How long would it take for him to lose himself? Would he even know when it happened?*

He was now alone. His parents would be part of the wall at the recycling centre, Kyle was sure. He tried to speak, and managed a small sound. He kept his thoughts alive by remembering his parents – or at least trying to. Memories kept slipping away from him, no matter how hard he tried to keep them.

Maybe it would have been better, he thought, *to have been with the last of the people from the Ordinary Settlement.* At least that way everything would have been quick. Part of him fought against this thinking; he still wanted to be human.

He wondered if the Organisation Rep could hear any of his thoughts in this room. 'Yes I can,' Kyle heard the Organisation Rep reply in his head. 'I'm enjoying this immensely, so please keep fighting.' Kyle wanted to cry, but no tears came.

Time slipped away from him. He had no idea how long he had been in the room and was beginning not to care. The part of him which still wanted to fight screamed inside his head.

He stared at the white walls, trying to imagine what it was like to be swallowed up. He wondered if he should walk into the wall and find out. He kept staring at the walls, his mind slowly fading away.

Suddenly he became aware of someone standing in front of him. It was his mum and dad! Kyle sprang to his feet and threw himself into their arms. They said they had come to take him back to the Ordinary Settlement, that everything was all right. The dirt he had thrown on the machines had worked. The Organisation was defeated. The final spark of humanity left in Kyle cried out with joy.

He was safe. He was going home. He was going to do whatever his parents told him to do from now on, and never be curious again.

He looked at his parents and saw them smiling happily at each other, the way they had before the Organisation came. Their happy, relaxed smiles and green glinting eyes.

Kyle blinked in shock. He took a careful look at them. Their eyes looked as normal as he expected them to look. They smiled reassuringly at him and led him out of the room.

He was safe… *wasn't he?*

About The Author

Claire Miller lives with her family in Glasgow, Scotland. She has been writing seriously since 2001. This is the first book she has published. As well as writing she enjoys spending her time singing, playing piano, drawing, designing cards either drawn or with materials and teaching adults how to use computers. She can be contacted at campsiehillsbooks@gmx.com.